The Witch Grows Up

Story and pictures by NORMAN BRIDWELL

SCHOLASTIC INC.

New York   Toronto   London   Auckland   Sydney

For Joshua

ISBN 0-590-40559-4

12 11 10 9 8 7 6 5 4 3 2 1   7 8 9/8 0 1 2/9

Printed in the U.S.A.   24
First Scholastic printing, August 1987

The lady who lives next door is a witch.
She is our friend.

One day we asked her, "What was it like when you were a little girl?"

She said her mother and father were
witches. They were glad when they knew
they were going to have a baby.

They made a special cradle for the new baby.

She had toys, dolls, and stuffed animals.

When her daddy came home, he would toss her into the air . . . .

When she didn't want to eat, her mother
had ways of getting her to eat.

She had a wading pool . . .

and a jungle gym.

Sometimes she would talk back to her mother and father.

She learned not to do that.

When she was a little older, she played
with other kids. She had her own jump rope.

She was good at tag.

Very good!

When the boys wouldn't let her
use their tree house . . .

she didn't care. The tree
was a friend of hers.

Her mother was like a lot of mothers. She wanted her little girl to take music lessons.

She listened to the little witch play her violin every day.

When the little witch was old enough,
she went to school.

She went to witch school.

All the little witches took cooking
lessons. They didn't make cupcakes.

They cooked up other things.

They studied spelling.

She learned some good spells.

And she learned to ride on a broom.

She was good at that.

When school was out she rushed home,
because that was the best place in the world.

Every night at bedtime her father
read her a story.

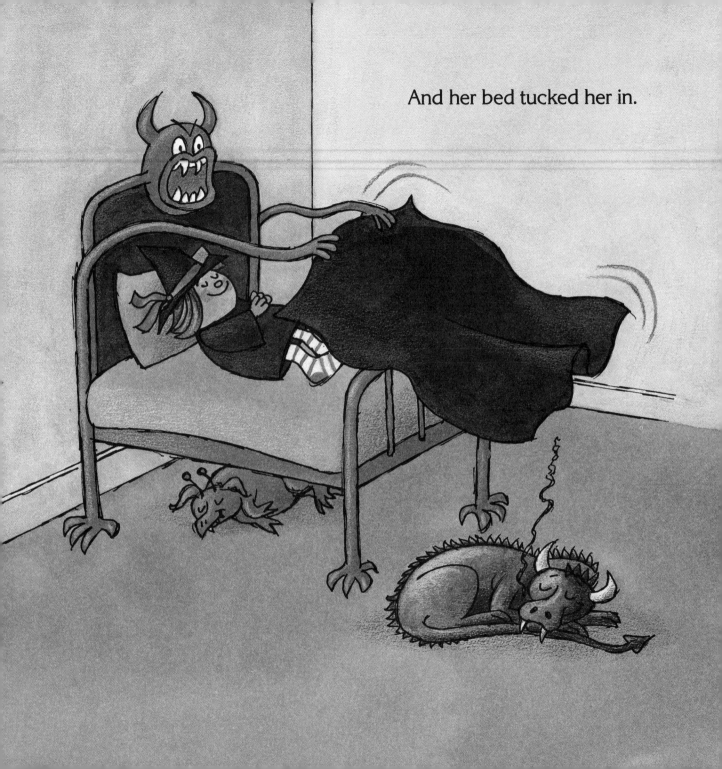

And her bed tucked her in.

The little witch had good dreams.

You see, little witches
are just like you and me.